For my **Nana Daisy**, a gentle, loving and wise woman. Nana faced much adversity in her life, yet retained her strength, dignity and humility. She always thought of others and made sure everyone was looked after. I loved all the time I spent with Nana wandering around the backyard, hearing her stories and laughing together. She taught me more than anyone and I am eternally grateful. I really loved Nana who remains in my heart forevermore.

CROW BABY

Helen Milroy

Long, long ago when the universe was newly created, there were times when special things could happen. These times were unpredictable and unique – anything was possible. Sometimes a strange glow would fill the sky like twilight and time itself seemed to slow down. It was during one of these times, that crow baby was born.

In the heavens a crow spirit was waiting to come down to the earth to take her place with the crow clan. But, because time had slowed, the spirit's journey was altered. Instead of arriving for the birth of a baby crow, the crow spirit arrived at the **birth of a human baby.**

When the baby was born, a strange glow surrounded the infant. No one knew what this meant but everyone knew it was very special.

Nearby the crow clan had gathered for the arrival of their baby crow, when they heard a strange sound. A human baby that not only cried like a baby but also **cawed like a crow.**

Suddenly the baby was not only surrounded by her family but by the entire crow clan. Nothing like this had ever happened before. The human family and the crow clan looked at each other in astonishment. **This child had been given the gift of two spirits: one crow, one human.**

'This is a very special baby indeed,' cawed an elder crow, pointing at a tuft of black hair at the back of the baby's head which resembled three feathers bundled together.

'Any crow born with three feathers like these is destined for great things. In the time of Creation the three feathers were given to the crows to symbolise courage, wisdom and kindness. These three things combined help us to stay strong together.'

The crow clan quickly realised their crow baby would have to grow up with her human family and the human family knew the crow clan would be important in their baby's life.

One of the oldest and wisest crows was given the task of looking after crow baby and would always stay close by just in case. The crow's name was Arrk, which in crow language means the keeper of knowledge. Arrk was one of very few crows who was born with the three special feathers at the back of the neck.

The human family accepted Arrk as her guardian and knew she would always be safe.

The human family talked with the crow clan about what to call crow baby. Together, they decided to wait for the right name to appear. They all lived in a forest surrounded by beautiful wildflowers. At dawn, crow baby would wake up and be ready for the day, full of hope and joy. At dusk crow baby would drift off into a deep sleep and dream peacefully.

'She only has an eye for the day,' said her father.

'Just like the wild daisies,' said her mother.

'Just like the crows,' cawed her guardian Arrk.

From then on, crow baby became known as **Daisy Crow.**

Daisy Crow grew with the years.

During the day, Daisy loved exploring the landscape, especially climbing trees to look out over the vast countryside with Arrk at her side. They spent many hours together talking and cawing about a great many things.

At night, when Daisy was asleep, her crow spirit would take flight and visit her families — both human and crow. The crow spirit always made sure to return to Daisy Crow before the first light.

Daisy Crow barely remembered her spirit journeys, until one morning after her mother had been very ill.

'Daisy,' her mother said, 'you visited me in my dreams. I'm sure it was you, but you were a crow sitting on the end of my bed talking to me! You brought me some eucalyptus leaves and sang me a sweet lullaby. When I awoke, I was feeling much better!'

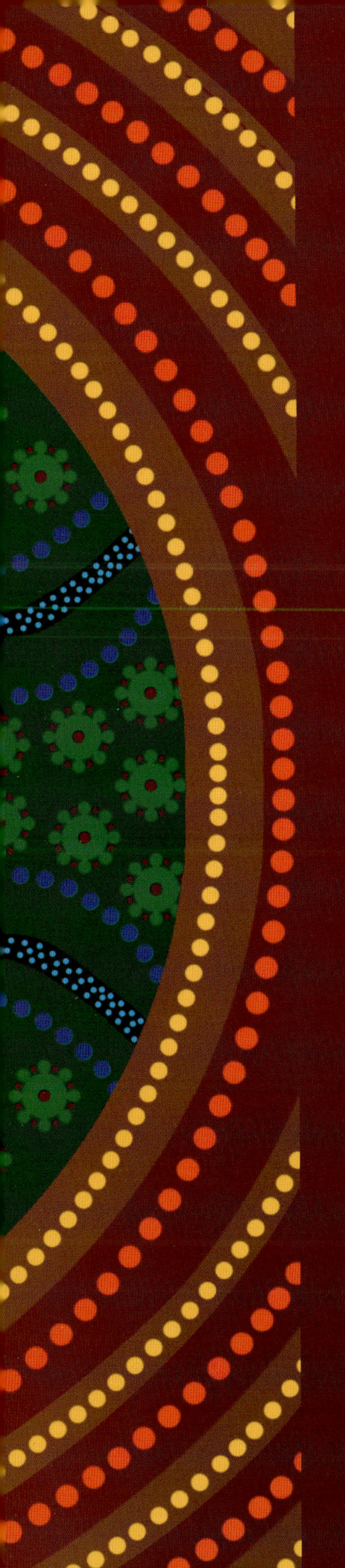

Daisy wasn't sure what to make of this. She decided to speak to the Elder. He was the oldest and wisest lawman in the community and a powerful healer.

Daisy Crow told the Elder about her mother's dream and also about other dream journeys Daisy had now begun to remember.

The Elder told Daisy Crow she had been given the gift of flight through her crow spirit. It was a powerful and precious gift, he said, and a sign she might become a great healer. But, he warned Daisy, she needed to be careful about how she used her gifts. **It was only safe to fly in her dreams.**

Daisy Crow continued to **grow** and **explore** and soon knew her way around Country. She was often off on long adventures learning about the bush medicines and how everything worked together.

One long, hot summer, the weather was scorching and the landscape had become dry and barren. Daisy Crow travelled out to see if she could find some new waterholes. Arrk warned Daisy not to go too far as the sun was in a fierce mood and had been causing small fires all day, but Daisy walked a long way from home. All of a sudden, a huge bushfire erupted across the landscape.

‘Run, Daisy, run,’ cawed Arrk.

Daisy was frightened and ran as fast as she could, but the fire was quickly catching up. It was heading towards her community and Daisy Crow knew she had to warn everyone.

‘You’ll have to fly,’ cawed her guardian loudly.

‘But I can’t, I don’t know how,’ cried Daisy. ‘Anyway, it is forbidden to fly outside my dreaming. I don’t know what will happen to me if I try!’

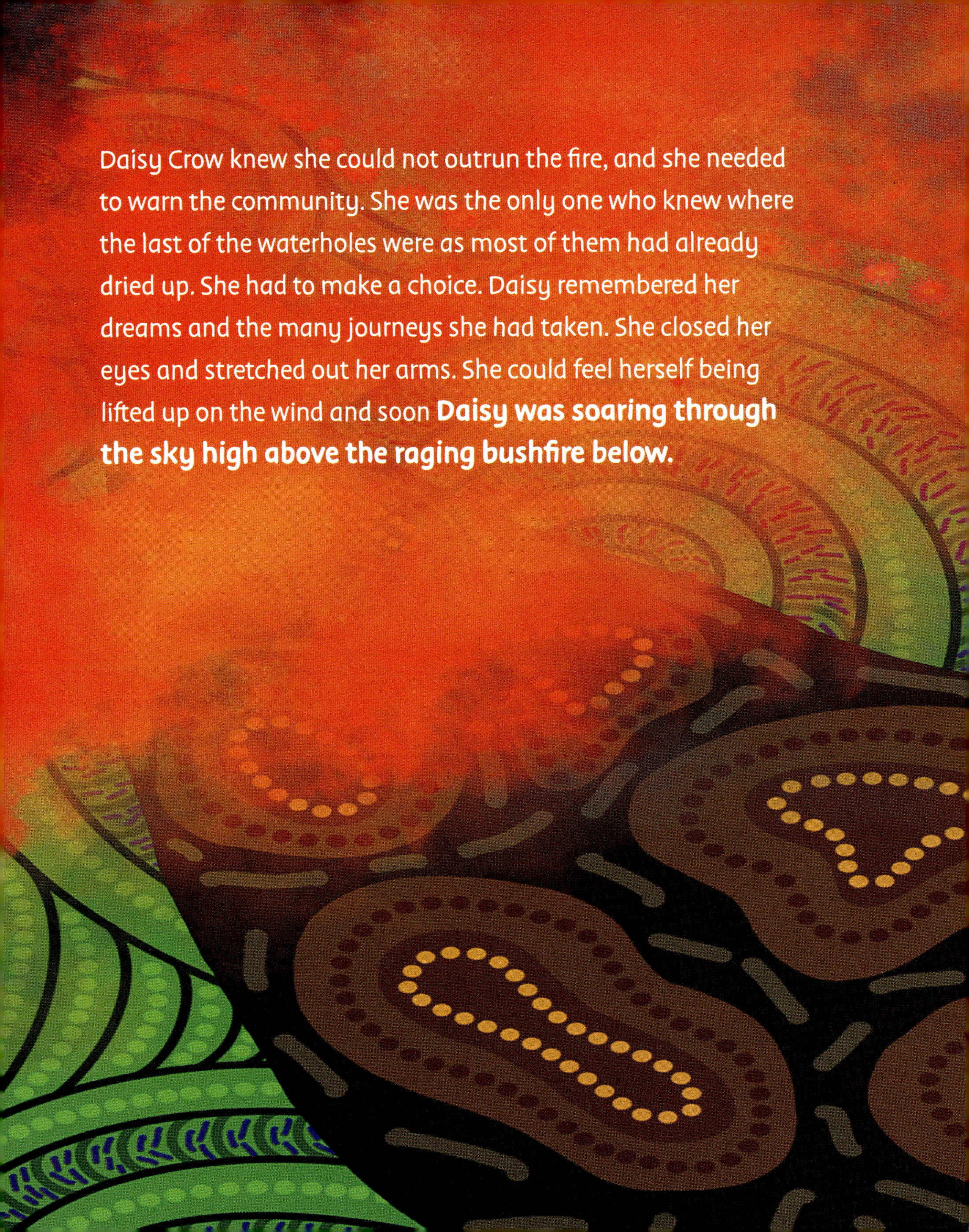

Daisy Crow knew she could not outrun the fire, and she needed to warn the community. She was the only one who knew where the last of the waterholes were as most of them had already dried up. She had to make a choice. Daisy remembered her dreams and the many journeys she had taken. She closed her eyes and stretched out her arms. She could feel herself being lifted up on the wind and soon **Daisy was soaring through the sky high above the raging bushfire below.**

As a crow, Daisy could easily fly ahead of the flames.

Daisy called and cawed loudly, warning everyone of what was coming. The whole community followed her to the waterhole knowing the fire could not cross its banks. Everyone was safe as the fire raged past them all burning everything in its wake. So much of the forest was burnt and left smouldering. It would take the forest a long time to heal.

'Daisy Crow,' shouted her mother,
'you have saved us all!'

The whole community surrounded Daisy Crow and looked on in astonishment. Although Daisy Crow was safe on the ground, she stood there proud and tall as a small black crow, talking and cawing as she had always done. Instead of the tuft of hair that resembled the three feathers, she now had long flowing feathers that resembled her beautiful black hair! Because Daisy Crow had taken flight outside of her dreaming, she would now remain in the form of a crow **forever.**

Everyone wept with tears of joy and sadness at what had become of Daisy Crow and the great sacrifice she had made. Her mother looked on knowing she would no longer hold her daughter as before. The crows gathered nearby and sang a mournful song to acknowledge what had taken place.

Later that day, Daisy Crow joined Arrk in the old gum tree near the waterhole. The crow clan gathered together to welcome her with a song that echoed across the landscape. They were overjoyed at the return of their crow baby.

As the sun set, Daisy settled into a nest and fell into a deep sleep. This time, it was her human spirit that awoke and made the long climb down from the tree, returning to the nest just in time for the dawn.

Daisy Crow was happy living with the crow clan. She loved **flying high in the sky** and travelling far and wide to collect her bush medicines. Daisy continued to make her healing journeys at night, but now in her human spirit.

The years passed, and Daisy did indeed become a great healer just as the Elder had predicted. And Daisy Crow's human family was always pleased to see her once again in human form, even if it was only in their dreams.

Helen Milroy is a descendant of the Palyku people of the Pilbara region of Western Australia. She was born and educated in Perth. Helen has always had a passionate interest in health and wellbeing, especially for children. Helen studied medicine at the University of Western Australia. She is currently a professor at UWA, Consultant Child and Adolescent Psychiatrist, Board Member with Beyond Blue and the AFL's first Indigenous Commissioner.